WAIT! Don't read that title!

to my teachers
past, present, and future

The Pigeon HAS to Go to School!

...res by mo willems

Hyperion Books for Children
New York
An Imprint of Disney Book Group

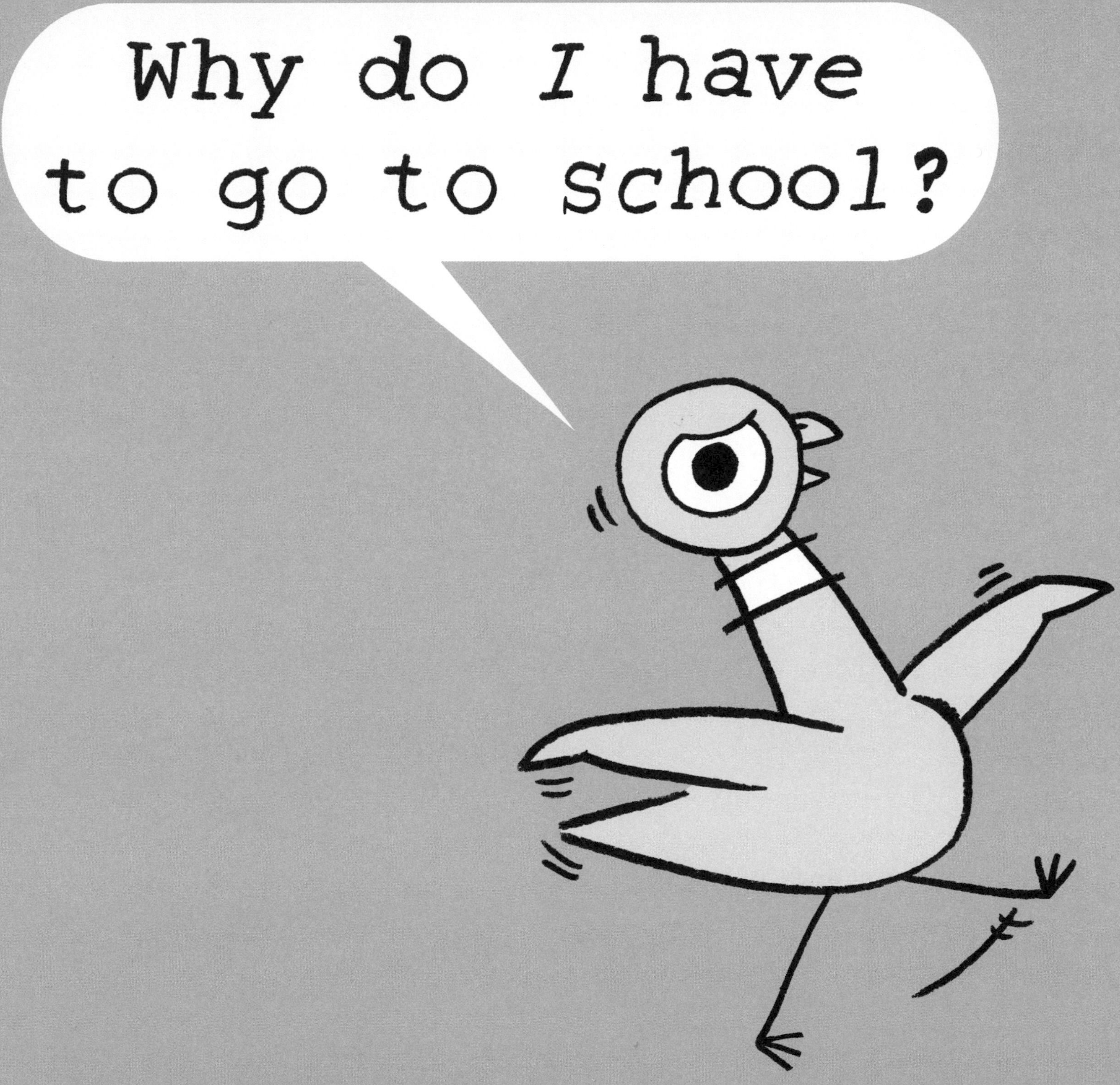
Why do *I* have to go to school?

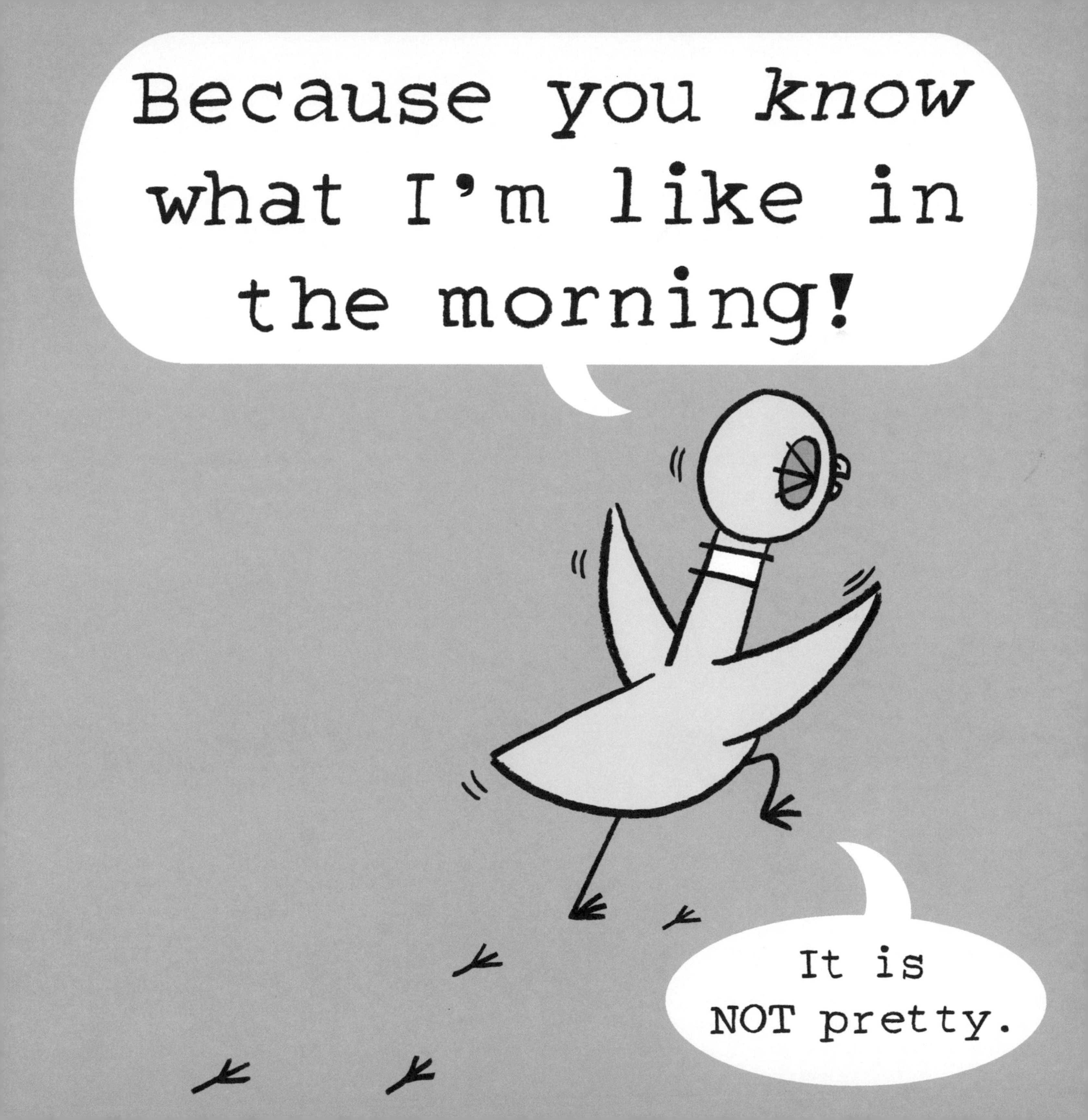
Because you *know* what I'm like in the morning!
It is NOT pretty.

I wish
I was
a little
chick
again.

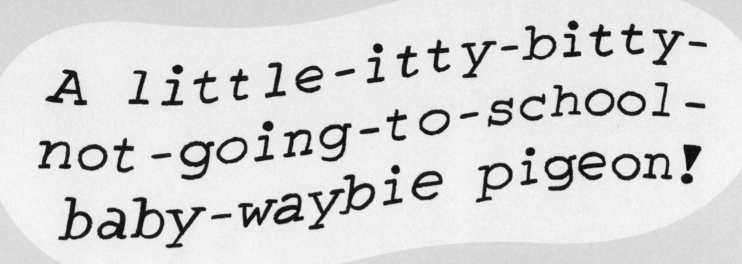

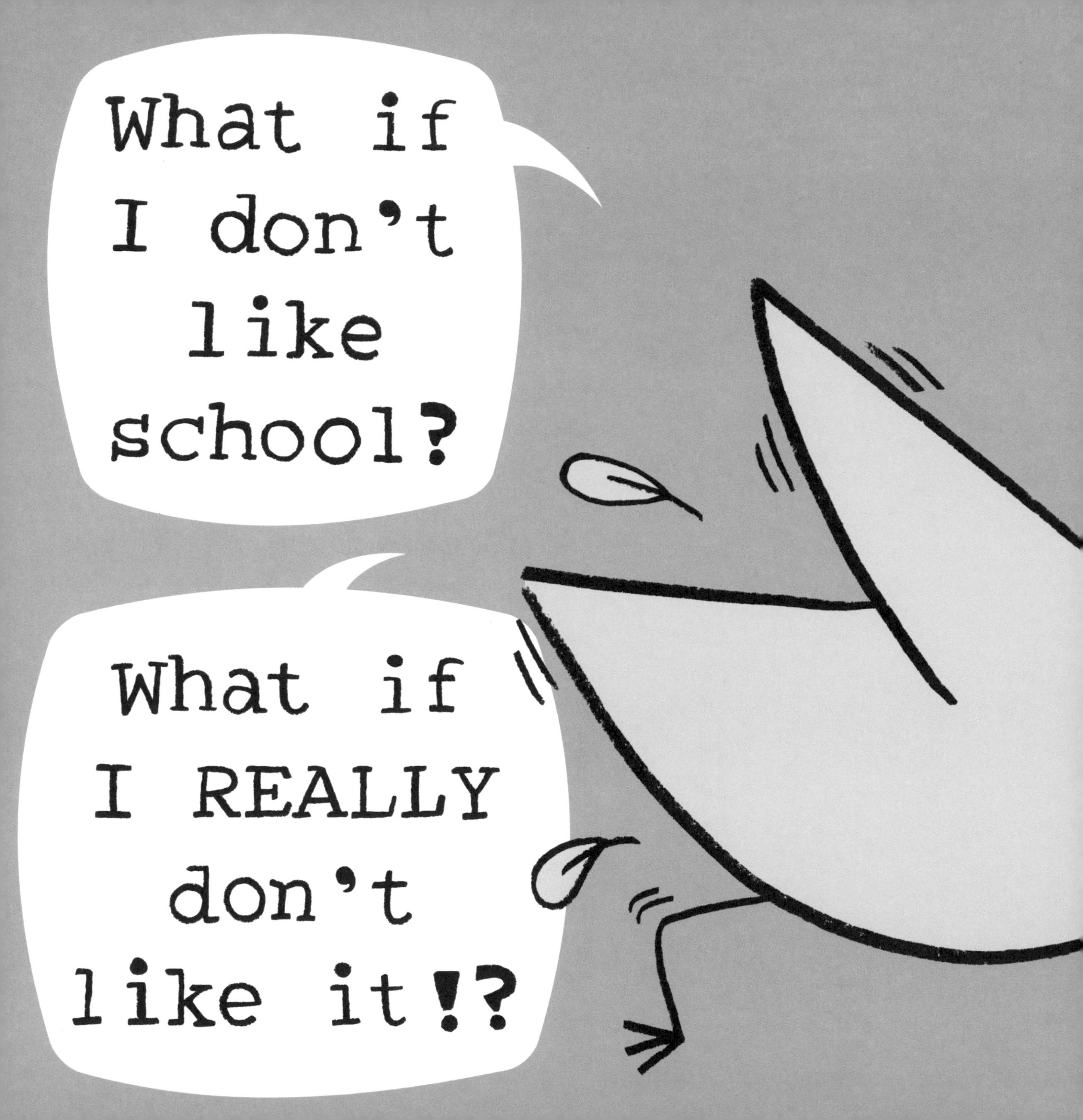
What if I don't like school?
What if I REALLY don't like it!?

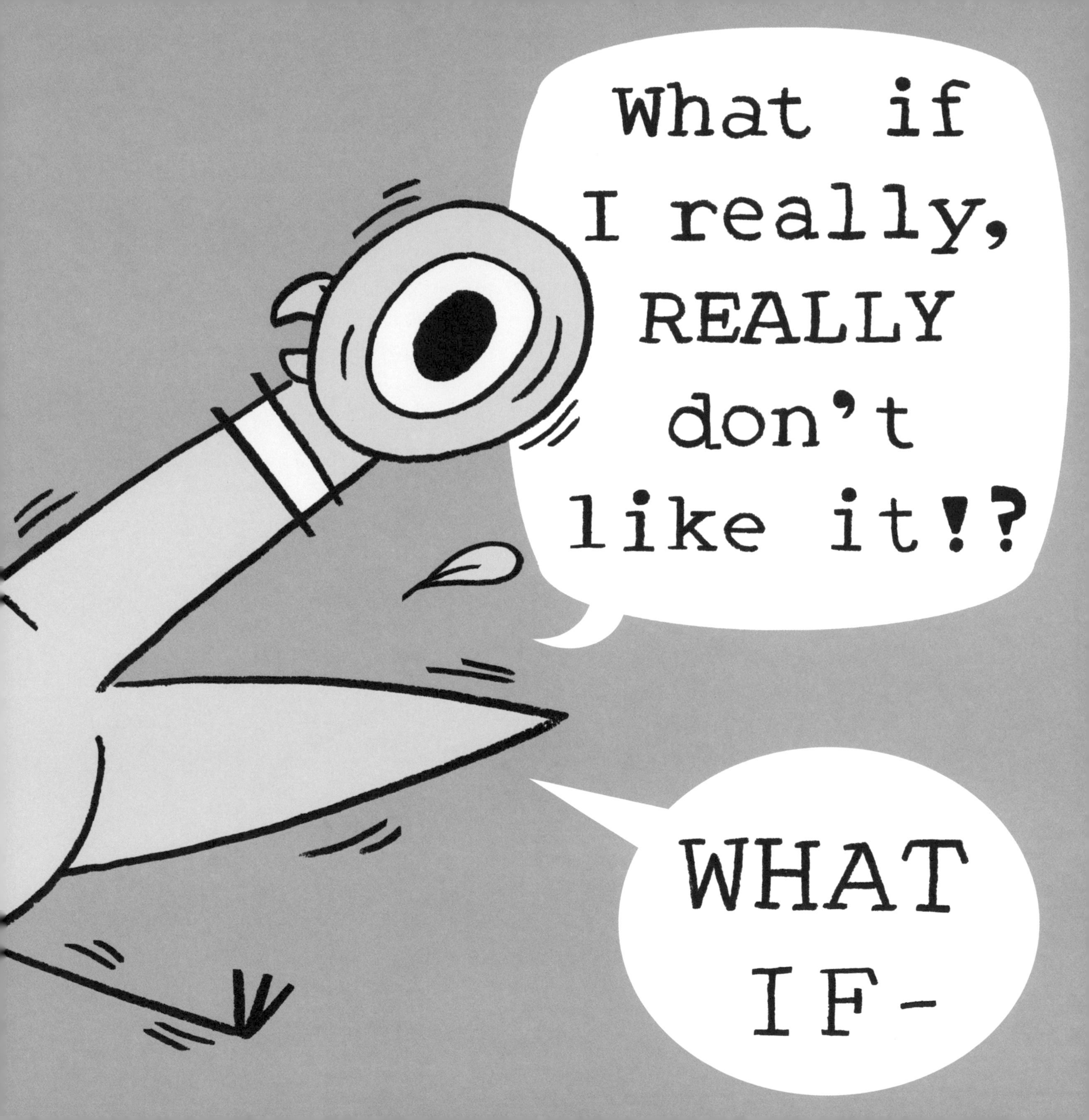
What if I really, REALLY don't like it!?
WHAT IF-

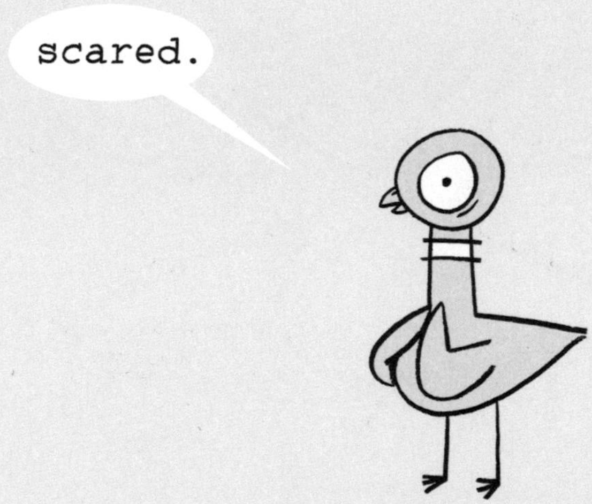
scared.

What if there is MATH?

Or numbers?

Why does the alphabet have so many LETTERS?!

READING can be hard with one big eye!

WHAT ABOUT LUNCH!?!

What will the other birds THINK of me?

Will FINGER PAINT stick to my feathers?

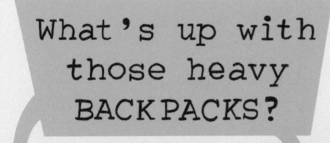

What's up with those heavy BACKPACKS?

I'm a fragile bird.

The unknown stresses me out, dude.

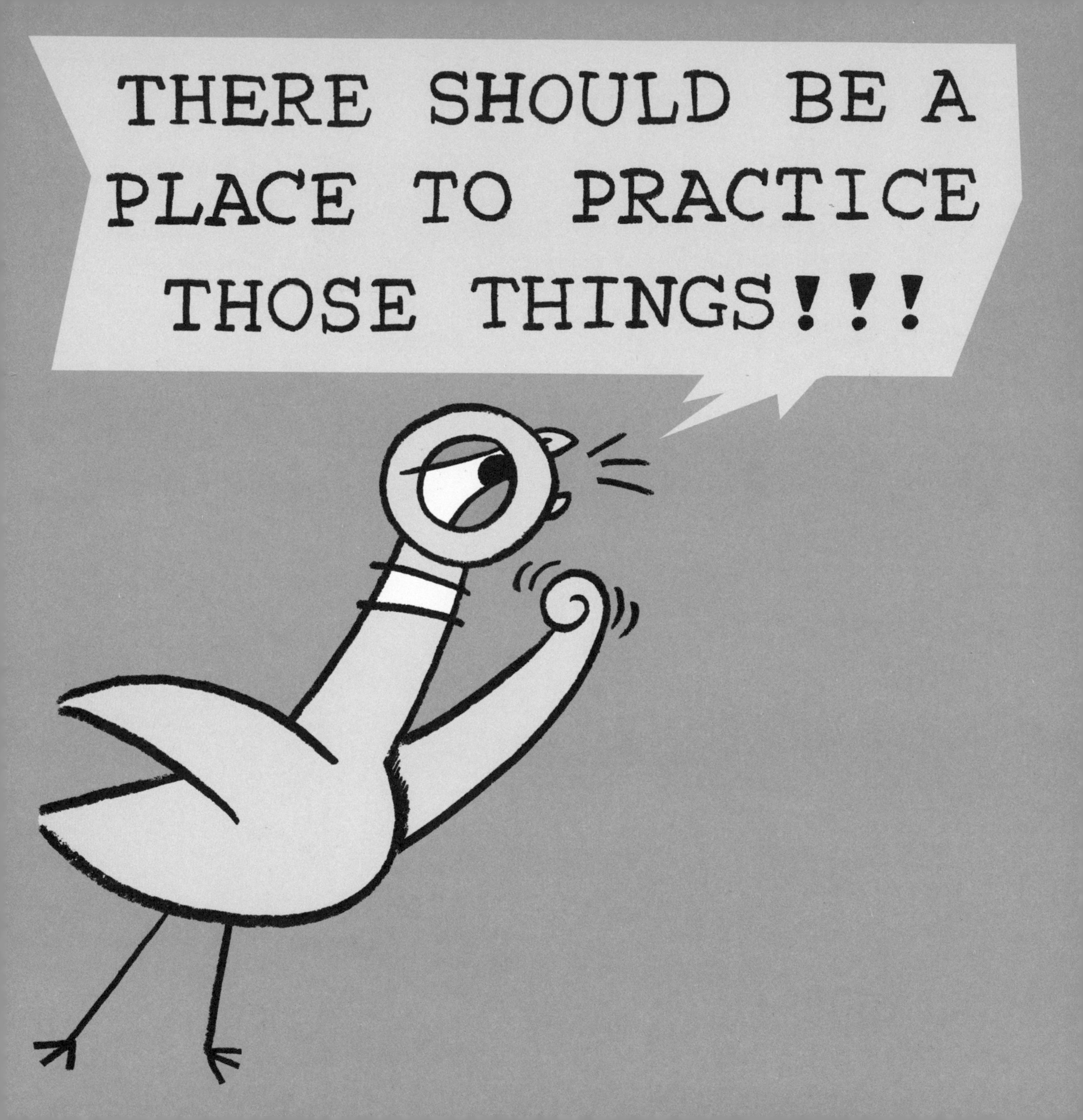
THERE SHOULD BE A PLACE TO PRACTICE THOSE THINGS!!!

With EXPERTS to help you.
And books.
And classrooms.
And other birds to work and play with.
Maybe a playground.

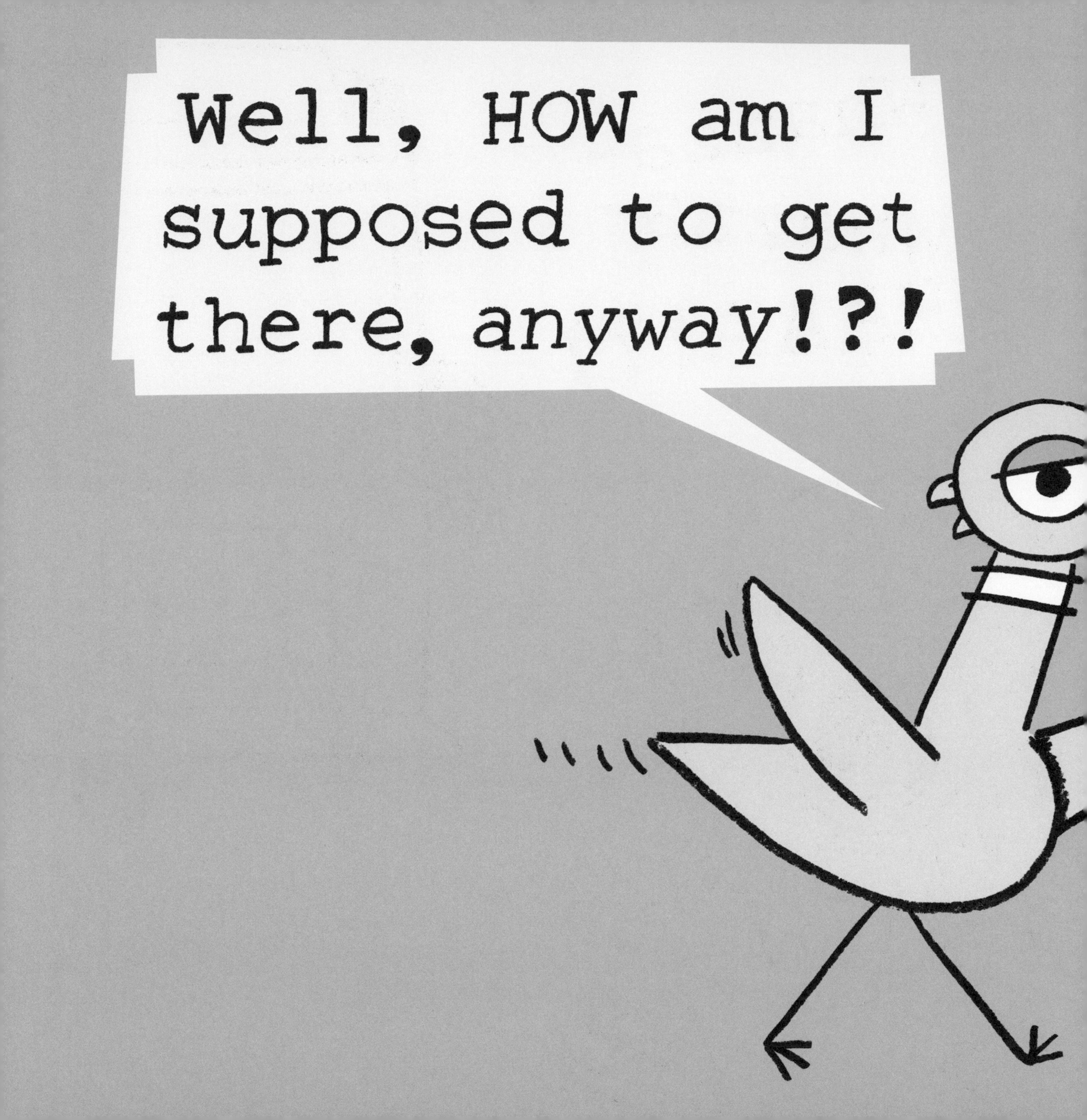
Well, HOW am I supposed to get there, anyway!?!

All rights reserved for humans, not pigeons. Published
by Hyperion Books for Children, an imprint of Disney
Book Group. No part of this book may be reproduced or
transmitted in any form or by any means, electronic or
mechanical, including photocopying, recording, or by any
information storage and retrieval system, without written
permission from the publisher. For information address
Hyperion Books for Children, 125 West End Avenue,
New York, New York 10023.

First Edition, July 2019
3 5 7 9 10 8 6 4 • FAC-034274-19333
Printed in the United States of America

This book is hand-lettered by Mo Willems, with
additional text set in Helvetica Neue LT Pro and
Latino Rumba/Monotype.

Reinforced binding

Visit www.hyperionbooksforchildren.com
and www.pigeonpresents.com

Library of Congress Cataloging-in-Publication Data

Names: Willems, Mo, author, illustrator.
Title: The pigeon has to go to school! / words and pictures
by Mo Willems. • Description: First edition. • New York :
Hyperion Books for Children, [2019] • Summary: The
Pigeon must go to school, but frets about math, learning the
alphabet, heavy backpacks, and what the teacher and other
birds will think of him. Identifiers: LCCN 2018033135 • ISBN
9781368046459 (hardcover) Subjects: • CYAC: First day
of school—Fiction. • Fear—Fiction. • Schools—Fiction. •
Pigeons—Fiction. • Humorous stories.
Classification: LCC PZ7.W65535 Pij 2019 • DDC [E]—dc23
LC record available at https://lccn.loc.gov/2018033135